Fun China

Our Chinese Hometown
The Fairy and the Tiger-head Shoes

Written by **Ada Ho How-sim**
Illustrated by **Sheung Wong**

Sun Ya Publications (HK) Ltd.
www.sunya.com.hk

Fun China

Our Chinese Hometown: The Fairy and the Tiger-head Shoes

Author
Ada Ho How-sim

Illustrator
Sheung Wong

Reviewer
Judith Malmsbury

Executive Editor
Tracy Wong

Graphic Designer
Karla Lau

Publisher
Sun Ya Publications (HK) Ltd.
18/F, North Point Industrial Building, 499 King's Road, Hong Kong
Tel: (852) 2138 7998 Fax: (852) 2597 4003
Website: https://www.sunya.com.hk
E-mail: marketing@sunya.com.hk

Distributor
SUP Publishing Logistics (HK) Ltd.
16/F, Tsuen Wan Industrial Centre, 220-248 Texaco Road,
Tsuen Wan, N.T., Hong Kong
Tel: (852) 2150 2100 Fax: (852) 2407 3062
E-mail: info@suplogistics.com.hk

Printer
C & C Offset Printing Co., Ltd.
36 Ting Lai Road, Tai Po, N.T., Hong Kong

Edition
First Published in August 2024

ISBN: 978-962-08-8446-7

About the Story

To everyone's surprise, the little fairy on Sunny's toy shelf has magical powers. To save Sunny's critically ill Grandpa, the little fairy awakens a pair of tiger-head shoes from Grandpa's childhood and unleashes their magical powers!

Let's read the story and cheer for Grandpa.

This afternoon, the house is quiet.
That is very strange!
Where are Mum and Dad?
Where is Sunny?
Where is Grandpa?

Yesterday, Grandpa was reading stories about days gone by and old customs to Sunny.

Sunny asked, "Do tiger-head shoes* really have magical powers?"

Grandpa nodded and smiled, "Yes, I have a pair myself."

* Tiger-head shoes (虎頭鞋) are a traditional Chinese folk handicraft for babies. They are made from wool. According to folk belief, these baby shoes protect a child's health and help them grow as robust as a tiger.

The next morning, Sunny's toy fairy wakes up.

Something has happened. She flies to the bookcase and knocks on the wall.

Knock, knock …

Knock, knock …

"Tiger-head shoes, wake up quickly! You have been asleep for decades. Wake up!"

Seventy years ago,
when Grandpa was born,
Great-grandma gave him
a pair of tiger-head shoes.
Great-grandma said,
"Tiger-head shoes, please
watch over my son."

From then on, wherever Grandpa went to study or work, he always brought the tiger-head shoes with him.

9

Ahh!

Ahh!

Upon hearing the little fairy's call, the
tiger-head shoes rub their sleepy eyes and
climb out of the storage box. They stretch
with two big yawns, "Ahh! Ahh!"

The fairy tells them, "This morning, Grandpa had a fall and was sent to the hospital. His condition is really critical!"

"What can we do? What can we do?" The tiger-head shoes shout anxiously.

"Tiger-head shoes, with your magical powers, protect your master!" the fairy orders them.

13

In the hospital, Grandpa is in a deep sleep. The whole family is worried.

"Grandpa, please wake up!" Sunny keeps asking him. Can he hear her?

三月
10

14

"Mum, will Grandpa wake up?" Sunny asks.
Mum has tears in her eyes and doesn't say a word.

"Dad, will Grandpa wake up?" Sunny asks.
Dad lowers his head and says, "I don't know.
Sunny, let's come visit Grandpa again tomorrow!"

Sunny suddenly
remembers what
Grandpa told her...

"Tiger-head shoes,
I found you! I found you!"
The tiger-head shoes say,
"Sunny, bring us to Grandpa, please!"

18

"Grandpa, you said the tiger-head shoes have magical powers. Here they are."
Sunny puts them in Grandpa's hands.

三月
11

19

Sunny says, "Grandpa, please wake up!"
But Grandpa is still deeply asleep.

"How can we wake him up?"
The tiger-head shoes are talking it over.
What will they do?

As night falls, and the hospital becomes
very quiet, the tiger-head shoes enter Grandpa's
dreams...

"Grandpa was once a cute
baby," they whisper.

"Wow! Grandpa had so much fun during the Chinese New Year!" they remind him.

The tiger-head shoes travel around the sweetest
memories of Grandpa's past.
Over and over they whisper to him, and tell him
they are with him.

The next day, Sunny returns to visit Grandpa.

"Grandpa, please wake up. I'm here to read you a story."

25

Three days later, Grandpa is sitting up.
Awesome! Sunny is so happy!

"Grandpa, look, the little tigers are dancing for you."

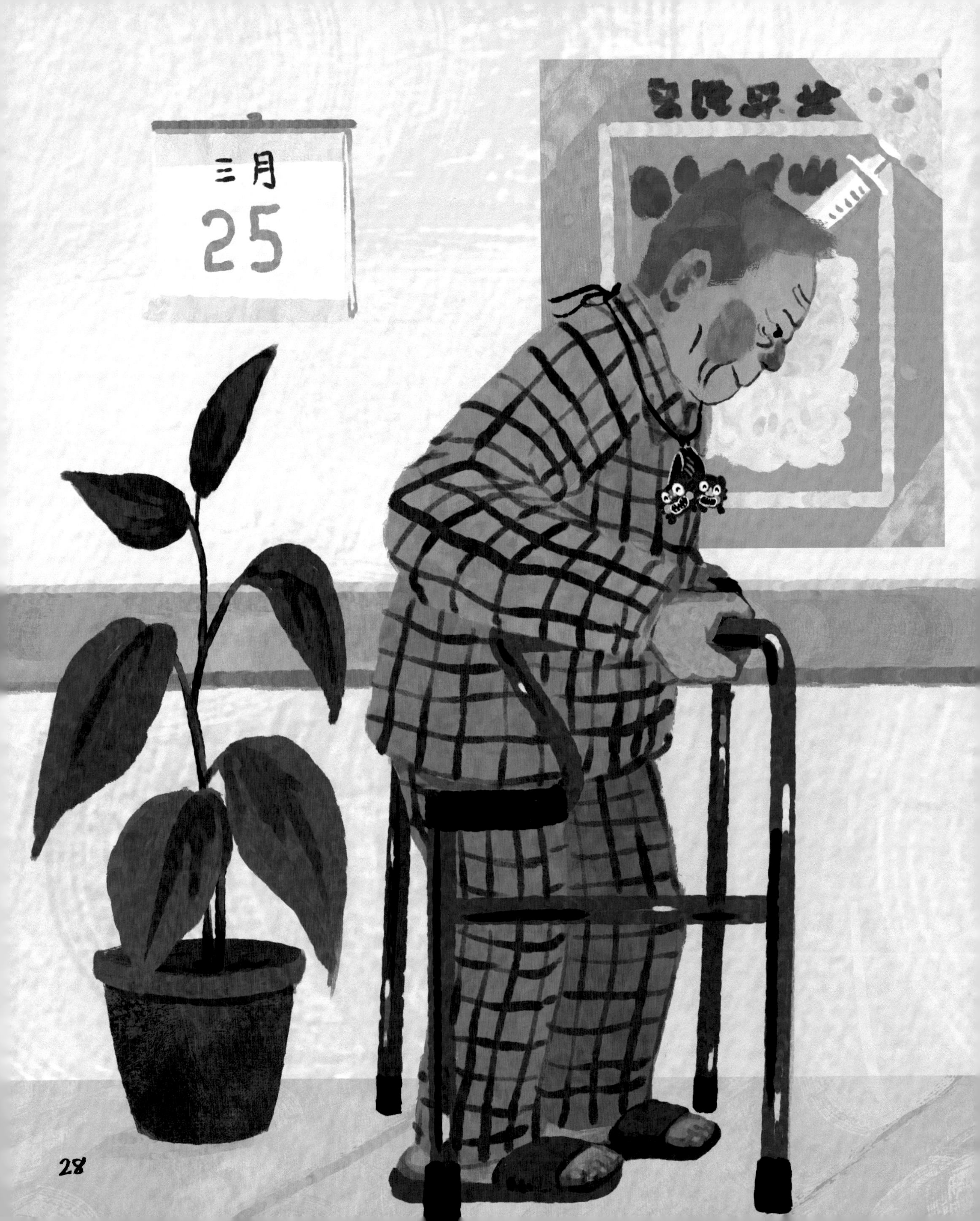
三月
25

Ten days later, Grandpa is learning to walk with the walker.
He tries very hard, and he makes a lot of effort.
He is tired, and Sunny cheers on Grandpa,
"One step at a time, that's the way!
Getting better day by day!"

The little tiger-head shoes whisper to him,
"Left and right, step by step,
Grandpa is the best!"

Today, Grandpa can finally
leave the hospital and go home.
Everyone can't help but cheer
together, "Home sweet home!"

Thank you, tiger-head shoes!

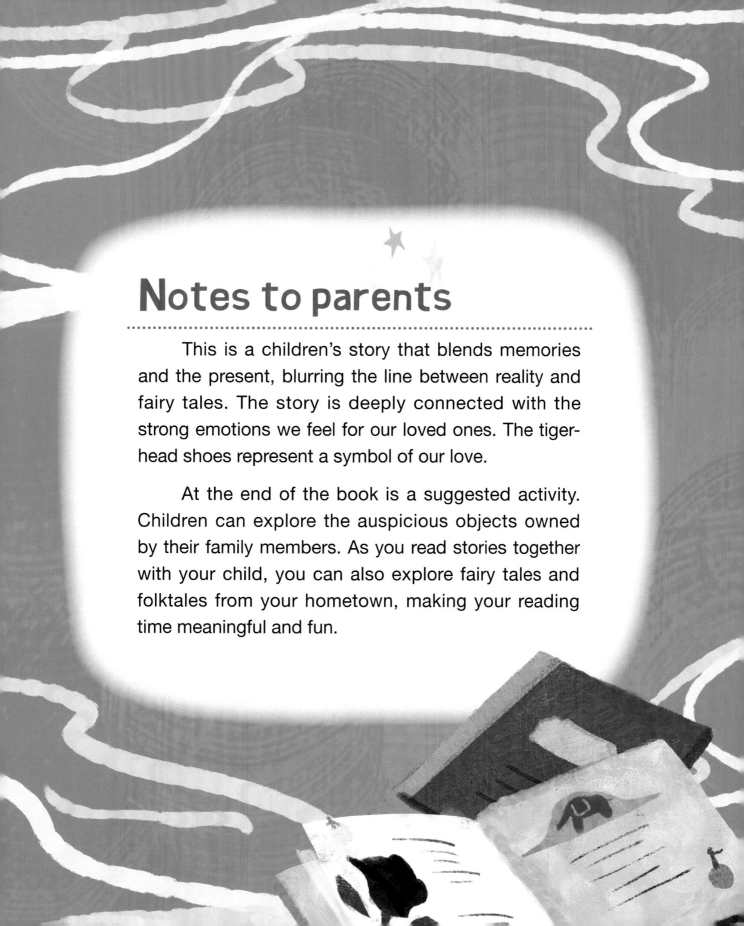

Notes to parents

This is a children's story that blends memories and the present, blurring the line between reality and fairy tales. The story is deeply connected with the strong emotions we feel for our loved ones. The tiger-head shoes represent a symbol of our love.

At the end of the book is a suggested activity. Children can explore the auspicious objects owned by their family members. As you read stories together with your child, you can also explore fairy tales and folktales from your hometown, making your reading time meaningful and fun.

Searching for Auspicious Objects

In many regions, the older generation often gives babies and small children small items with auspicious meanings as gifts, hoping that they will have magical power to protect the children's health and growth. These objects come in various forms. Some are wearable items such as the little tiger-head shoes in the story, while others are not.

Let's ask your family members the following questions to see if anyone has received an auspicious gift.

1. Do you have an auspicious item?

_____

2. Who gave it to you?

_____

3. What do you use it for?

_____

4. Do you know any folk stories related to it?

_____

You may ask more questions and write down the answers in a notebook. You can also take photos or draw pictures of them to record these precious memories of your family.

About the Author

Ada Ho How-sim

Ada Ho is an Honorary Fellow of The Education University of Hong Kong. She holds a master's degree in Education from Macquarie University, Australia. She is a former principal and currently works as a writer, school director and guest lecturer at The Education University of Hong Kong.

In addition to her educational roles, Ada has held various public service positions, including school manager positions in different schools. She has also served as a professional consultant on literature and arts for the Leisure and Cultural Services Department of Hong Kong. She was also the former president of the Hong Kong Children's Literature Association.

Ada is committed to promoting children's reading and possesses a profound understanding of and concern for children's growth and development. As of 2024, she has published more than 180 books.

About the Illustrator

Sheung Wong

Sheung Wong is a talented illustrator from Hong Kong. Despite being born deaf, her passion for drawing has been with her since childhood. Graduating with a master's degree in Printmaking from the Guangzhou Academy of Fine Arts, Sheung combines printmaking, the pencil and chalk textures with digital techniques. She has been creating illustrations for various companies and publishers since 2014.